First Edition 10 9 8 7 6 5 4 3 2
ISBN 978-1-4847-1495-9
FAC-025393-16004
Library of Congress Control Number: 2014943237

Printed in China

Visit www.disneybooks.com

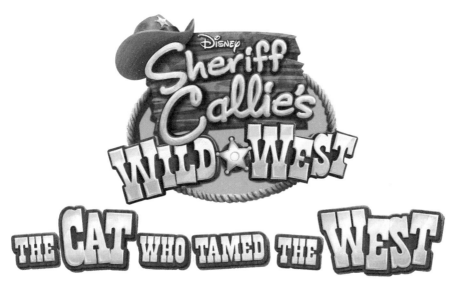

THE CAT WHO TAMED THE WEST

Written by Holly Huckins

Illustrated by Marco Bucci

DISNEP PRESS
New York • Los Angeles

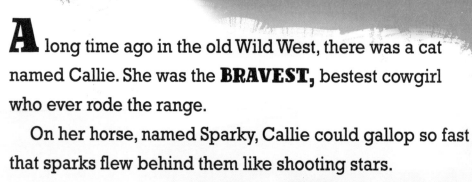

A long time ago in the old Wild West, there was a cat named Callie. She was the **BRAVEST,** bestest cowgirl who ever rode the range.

On her horse, named Sparky, Callie could gallop so fast that sparks flew behind them like shooting stars.

And with her magic **NOODLE LASSO,** she could rope a twister and ride it like a bronco in a rodeo ring.

One morning, Callie and Sparky took off on a fun ride.
"WOO-WEE!" said Callie. "I've worked up a mighty **BIG THIRST.**"
Sparky was thirsty, too, so they headed off to find something to drink.

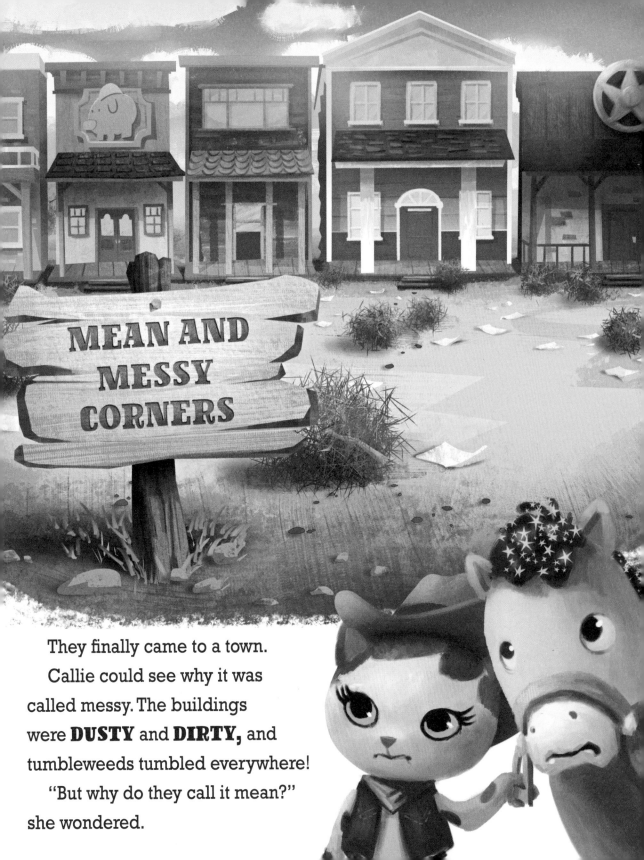

MEAN AND MESSY CORNERS

They finally came to a town. Callie could see why it was called messy. The buildings were **DUSTY** and **DIRTY,** and tumbleweeds tumbled everywhere!

"But why do they call it mean?" she wondered.

As Callie walked down the street, she saw some townsfolk cleaning up. A **WOODPECKER** named Peck was sweeping with two brooms at once.

"HI-YA!" he hollered.

Toby the **CACTUS** was picking up paper with his spines. "I'm a prickly cowpoke," he said.

"**HOWDY, PARDNERS!** Know where I can get a nice cold glass of milk?" said Callie.

The little cat scared everybody! Mr. Dillo curled up in a **BALL,** Priscilla hid under her **PARASOL,** and Peck was so frightened he jumped into Toby's arms! **"OUCHITY-OUCH!"** yelled Peck. Toby's spines were sharp!

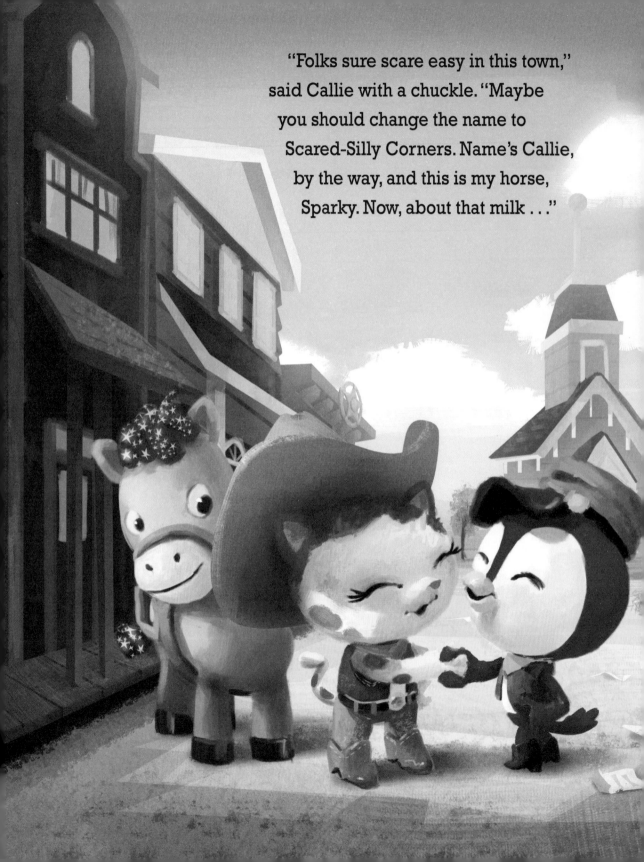

"Folks sure scare easy in this town," said Callie with a chuckle. "Maybe you should change the name to Scared-Silly Corners. Name's Callie, by the way, and this is my horse, Sparky. Now, about that milk . . ."

Peck and Toby said she'd find the
best milk in the West at **ELLA'S SALOON.**

"HOWDY, PARDNER!"

said Callie as she entered the **SALOON.**

Ella let out a funny yelp and hid behind the counter.

"Don't be afraid," said Callie. "There's nothing scary about me.
I'd just like a nice cold glass of milk!"
Ella laughed, feeling a little embarrassed, and said:
"COMING RIGHT UP."

Just then, a milk bandit barged into the saloon.

"PAWS UP! THIS IS A MILK RAID!"

"AAAAHHH!" cried Ella, hiding behind the counter again.

But Callie wasn't afraid. She whipped out her magic noodle lasso...

and bounced the milk bandit out of town before he could steal a drop. "And don't ever come back!" shouted Callie.

Ella was so **GRATEFUL** she gave
Callie an extra-big glass of milk.
"We don't usually get friendly folks passing
through—just the mean and messy ones," she said.
"That's why the town is called Mean and Messy Corners."

No sooner did Ella say this than two more
BANDITS rode into town.

"We're the **BANJO BANDIT BROTHERS**!"
shouted the big one. "Give us all yer banjos!"

The townsfolk got scared and ran away.

Uncle Bun jumped inside a barrel.

His friend Tío Tortuga hid inside his shell.

THE THREE PRAIRIE DOGS
tried to jump into their holes, but
one wasn't fast enough and the
big Banjo Bandit Brother
stole his **BANJO**!

Callie had seen enough.
She jumped on her horse
and cried out,

"GIDDYUP,
SPARKY!

We've got a banjo to save!"

And faster than you can say **"YEE-HAW!"** Callie gave those two bad brothers the boot and saved the banjo, too!

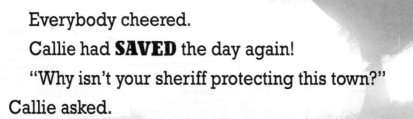

Everybody cheered.

Callie had **SAVED** the day again!

"Why isn't your sheriff protecting this town?"

Callie asked.

"Everybody is afraid to take the **SHERIFF** job," Peck told her. "And these bad guys keep coming back."

Suddenly, a stagecoach rode into town. The
BANDITS were back. They ran into the bank shouting,
"This is a **STICKY-UP**! Give us all your money!"

"OH, NO!" said Callie. She raced into the bank
to stop them, and when she did, a fourth bandit popped
out of the stagecoach and stole **SPARKY!**

But Callie wasn't worried.
She took her **NOODLE LASSO**
and spun it so fast the wind
twirled into a

TWISTER!

Callie rode that twister
like it was a buckin' bronco,
chasing down that horse thief
and saving Sparky.

Thanks to some extra-fancy twirling, she caught the rest of the bandits and put them all in jail.

"WHEE DOGGIE!" said Peck. "You did it!
You rid our town of bad guys!"

"I was right **HAPPY** to help," said Callie. "Especially
seeing as you don't have a sheriff and all."

"Why don't you be our **SHERIFF**?" asked Toby.

"Me?" said Callie. "Well, I'd love to."

"You'll need a badge," said Peck.

"A nice, shiny one," Toby added.

Sparky gave Callie a nudge and said, **"NEIGH!"**

"I think I can handle that,"

Callie replied with a wink.

So Callie took her magic lasso and spun it so fast and high that it plucked a star right out of the sky, and she pinned it on her vest.

That's how Callie became the **BEST** sheriff in the whole Wild West.
And that's how a little **TOWN** got itself
a brand-new name...

NICE AND
FRIENDLY
CORNERS.